D1095800

Big Heart!

A Valentine's Day Tale

By Joan Holub
Illustrated by Will Terry

Ready-to-Read • Aladdin
New York London Toronto Sydney

For Sandi Studans –J. H.

For Sosha and Avery –W. T.

ALADDIN PAPERBACKS
An imprint of Simon & Schuster Children's Publishing Division
1230 Avenue of the Americas, New York, NY 10020
Text copyright © 2007 by Joan Holub
Illustrations copyright © 2007 by Will Terry

Also available in an Aladdin library edition.
Designed by Lisa Vega.
The text of this book was set in Century Oldstyle BT.
Manufactured in the United States of America.
First Aladdin Paperbacks edition December 2007
2 4 6 8 10 9 7 5 3 1
Library of Congress Cataloging-in-Publication Data
Holub, Joan.
Big heart! : a Valentine's Day tale / by Joan Holub ;
illustrated by Will Terry. — 1st Aladdin Paperbacks ed.
p. cm. — (Ant Hill) (Ready-to-read)
Summary: Young ants are hard at work in their classroom making
a big valentine, but then they must decide on the recipient.
1. Valentines—Fiction. 2. Valentine's Day—Fiction. 3. Schools—Fiction.
4. Ants—Fiction. 5. Stories in rhyme.] I. Terry, Will, 1966- ill. II. Title.
PZ8.3.H74Bi 2007 [E]—dc22 2007015749
ISBN-13: 978-1-4169-0957-6 (pbk.) ISBN-10: 1-4169-0957-5 (pbk.)
ISBN-13: 978-1-4169-2562-0 (Library binding) ISBN-10: 1-4169-2562-7 (Library binding)

"Big heart,"
said Bart.

"Paint it," said Kit.

"Use red,"
said Fred.

"Glue stars,"
said Lars.

"Add lace," said Grace.

"How great!" said Kate.

"How cool!" said Jewel.

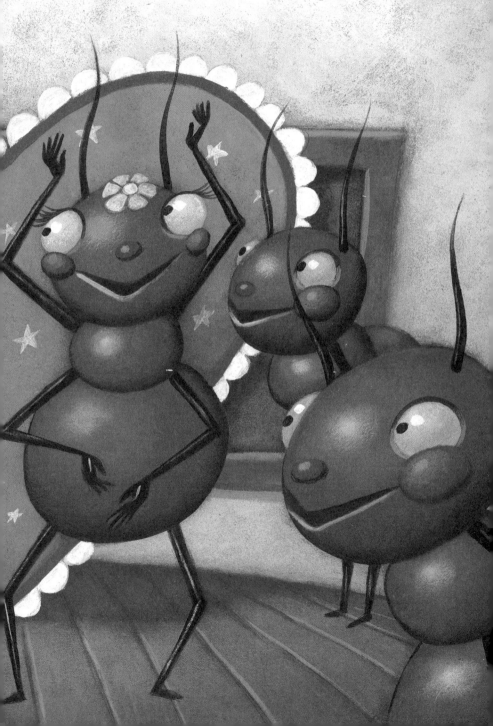

"For me?"
asked Lee.

"No way!"
said Jay.

"Mail it," said Kit.

"Who to?"
asked Drew.

"My mom!" said Tom.
"My dad!" said Brad.

"My aunt!" said Grant.
"My gran!" said Jan.

"Oh my,"
said Guy.

"Hard choice,"
said Joyce.

"Hard work," said Kirk.
"For him?" asked Jim.

"Bingo!" said Joe.

For you,
wrote Drew.

From us,
wrote Gus.

"Big smile," said Kyle.

"Big hearts,"
said Mr. Smarts.